MISSION
CHAOS

The North West

Edited By Kelly Reeves

First published in Great Britain in 2019 by:

Young Writers
Remus House
Coltsfoot Drive
Peterborough
PE2 9BF
Telephone: 01733 890066
Website: www.youngwriters.co.uk

All Rights Reserved
Book Design by Jenni Harrison
© Copyright Contributors 2019
Softback ISBN 978-1-83928-499-1
Hardback ISBN 978-1-83928-500-4
Printed and bound in the UK by BookPrintingUK
Website: www.bookprintinguk.com
YB0424N

FOREWORD

Survival Log: Day 52

We had almost lost hope. Disasters befell the earth and chaos reigned; we didn't think there were many survivors, if any. Here at Young Writers we sent out a call, a signal to anyone out there to communicate and let us know that we weren't alone. It seemed like a lost cause.

But then something miraculous happened.

We received thousands of messages – tales of destruction and danger, stories of survival against the odds, and devastating accounts of disasters both natural and man-made wreaking havoc upon the land. Not all of them have a happy ending, but all of them offer a blazing beacon of hope that secondary school pupils across the land are keeping their creativity alive.

Communications had to be kept to 100 words, but even with this restraint they've created vivid descriptions, powerful imagery and epic tales of the fight for survival; the fight for humanity. These stories have been collected in this anthology to serve as a lasting record of the chaos that raged across the globe, and how we fought back.

Every author featured should be proud in the vital part they've played in creating these Survival Sagas. I declare Mission Chaos a success.

Signing off,

Kelly

CONTENTS

Ronnie Pelech (12)   67

Fazakerley High School, Aintree

Georgia Nelson	68
Shannon Elizabeth Hamilton (13)	69
Chloe Jessica Hilton (13)	70
Karim Sumanschi (12)	71
Brodie Elizabeth Gardiner (13)	72
Harry James Williams (12)	73
Emma Navin (13)	74
Ruby Cleaton (12)	75
Michael Andrew Wright (13)	76
Lucy Oates	77
Joseph Arands (13)	78
Thomas Wilson (12)	79

Little Lever School, Little Lever

Lucy Edwards (11)	80
Ella Morley (12)	81
Zak Colman (11)	82
Eshaan Yaser (13)	83
Keira Howard	84
Ruben Worthington (13)	85
Ellie Louise Steane (12)	86
Maddison Dawson (12)	87
Nicole Lomas (12)	88
Lexie Grant (12)	89
Lucy Jane Willett (12)	90
Alyssa Hall (12)	91
Wahib Butt (13)	92
Finley Schofield (12)	93
Olivia Vining (14)	94
Lewis Martland (13)	95
Jack Ellis Walton (14)	96
Leah Lewis	97
Harley Johnson	98
Jacob Wiggins (14)	99
Ellie Louise Mottershead (13)	100
Michael Paul Bithell (12)	101
Tom Hamlett (13)	102
Kristian Taylor (14)	103

Callum Murray (14)	104
Sophia Magari (12)	105
Caden Jones (14)	106
Sophie Martin (13)	107
Bethany Cain (12)	108
Abby Gallagher (11)	109
Leon Jaydon Robert Tennant (12)	110
Isla Marisa Jones (12)	111
Ellis Matthews (14)	112
Tilly-Anne Wilson (12)	113
Sarah Ashworth (12)	114
Harry Owens	115
Bettina Balic (14)	116
Matthew Cowcill (14)	117
Louie Higgins	118
Sophie Gorman (14)	119
Charlotte Commons (12)	120
Cameron Welsby (12)	121
Josh Taylor (13)	122
Adam Marshall (14)	123
Ashleigh Jade May (13)	124
Sam Percival (14)	125
Kaine Larkin (12)	126
Harley Irwin (13)	127
Shane Naughton (14)	128
Grace Harwood (12)	129
Neve Warren (12)	130
Abby Rose Barratt (12)	131
Harrison Evans (14)	132
Lucy Jones (13)	133
Callum Lane (14)	134
Molly Walkden (14)	135
Kian Walmsley (11)	136
Jessica Alice Ramsden (12)	137
Caitlin Rhead (13)	138
Hanna Goodwin (12)	139
Lucy Grime (14)	140
Atta Rehman (13)	141
Grace Gavin (12)	142
Naomi Barber	143
Mia Conway (13)	144
Isabelle Greeney (12)	145

Kelsey-Jo Frost   146

Neston High School, Neston

Lucas Stephen Green (12)	147
Alfie Elliott Fisher (13)	148
Ben Downham (12)	149
Caroline Ross (12)	150

St Julie's Catholic High School, Woolton

Olivia Florence Long (13)	151
Daisy Darmody (13)	152
Ruby Kidd	153
Heather Langton (14)	154
Emma Robinson (11)	155
Amelia Leather	156
Ava McCutcheon	157
Caitlin Mottram (14)	158
Liv Ellis	159
Ava Dawes	160
Lexi Russell	161

THE
MINI SAGAS

The Patient Dystopia

"Follow me," it whispered. A continuous alarm airily dispersed my surroundings. It was leading me somewhere. Where? Suddenly, it dramatically appeared, eyes bloodshot with agony, ears pointed with sharp resent, the ebony-black silhouette increased the distress factor.

"Quick! I've waited long enough!" the figure retorted, responding to my gestures.

My eyes reluctantly scrapped the rickety oak floor. A cloud of white appeared, children playing joyfully. A *crash!* A boy walking in the streets, anticipating nothing. Old times rewound... A whirlwind of calamity acquainted my mind. I remembered, about three years ago, I murdered, I killed. He was back for revenge!

Zahara Idriss Maide (13)

All Saints Catholic College, Dukinfield

Brightness Into Life

Everywhere was in darkness! Darkness surrounded the towering buildings and what was the peaceful, beautiful countryside. The sky was pitch-black and shadowy and the lights were out. Total darkness filled the entire world. Suddenly, out of nowhere, a bright light burst from the horizon, sending sparks into life. The shimmering light shone straight into our eyes, making us fill with hope, happiness and kindness. Unexpectedly, in the countryside, the lovely sweet-smelling flowers beautifully blossomed into life. The flowers gracefully danced across the silent, calm meadow. The sapphire-blue ocean rippled in the cool, relaxing breeze.

Winnie Chen (13)
All Saints Catholic College, Dukinfield

Wipe Out

We're forbidden from entering the Dead Space. Inside, the dystopian, sinister leader, known as Agent 504, was torturing all the humans who survived: a homicidal maniac, his dastardly plan was to wipe out the entire human race single-handedly. So far, he had succeeded in slaughtering everyone. Everyone except for us. I peered inside, desperate to find a way to help them, and what I saw was petrifying. Several malicious machines began decapitating unsuspecting, innocent people, it was traumatising.

I opened the window and howled, "Stop!"

He had found me. We were the only ones left, or were we? Who knew?

Piper Jackson (13)
All Saints Catholic College, Dukinfield

Chaos

The machines marched, the war had begun. A high-pitched, flamboyant scream echoed in the serene surroundings. His hands cupped his ears and the reverberation elapsed. An eruption of deep crimson leapt into the air, crashing onto the floor. Hissing and crackling arose from deep underground: everything was burning. Below his feet, corpses rotted, releasing a horrifying smell of flesh decaying, it swept into mid-air and into the nose of the immature schoolboy looking for an adventure. Colossal buildings dropped like dead flies onto the dusty floor. At the end of the winding path, a drop formed abruptly. Everything disappeared!

Sophie Goode (13)
All Saints Catholic College, Dukinfield

Silence In The Woods

A bright light burst from the horizon as I ventured deeper into the desolate woods. Anxiously looking around, I acknowledged my surroundings as I watched the towering trees that guarded the woods retreat as they accepted their defeat. Recounting the events that had just occurred, I remembered the chemicals gushing out of the lab, crawling onto the streets. Rancid chemicals devoured everyone. Now, I wandered the long, winding streets that had long been abandoned as one question ran across my mind: *am I the only one left?*

Contemplating whether to carry on, an eerie whisper called out, "I see you..."

Zaara Karim (13)
All Saints Catholic College, Dukinfield

Alone

We were the only ones left... The screams outside demolished into silence. The menacing storm clouds gathered over the distant horizon. Confused, shocked, frightened, where had it gone? The vicious, violent creature could sense the fear surrounding me. Exhausted and worried, cold and startled, I didn't think I could survive any longer. Terrified, I instantly froze on the spot. I looked around, desperately searching for an escape... A flashback came upon me of losing my valuable, treasured mother. What if she was lost? Trapped? Captured? It was both unimaginable and unpleasant. I had known it had been the very end.

Heira Iqbal (13)
All Saints Catholic College, Dukinfield

The New Horizon

A bright light burst from the horizon of the battlefield of our society. Aggravatingly, our once responsible world leaders had been brainwashed by money, they became dominant and obsessive, leaving their hopeless citizens stranded in the dark and miserable abyss we called home. In every neighbourhood, gunshots were fired to signal us into coming out of hiding, to them we weren't people. We were objects. We were prisoners. Even our unswept shadows were deprived and hungry. After miles of running, I discovered a tranquil sanctuary away from my juvenile troubles and a place to recreate civilisation, once and for all!

Laila Henniker (12)
All Saints Catholic College, Dukinfield

Chernobyl

Smoke engulfed him as he sprinted from his inevitable fate. Sirens echoed around the desolate wasteland of the rundown nuclear powerplant. Adrenaline pumped into his veins, as his golden-brown skin began to melt away from his quartz-like bones. Nuclear waste cascaded from the unstable ceiling, he knew his final moments were coming to an end. The torturous pain became more unbearable with every consecutive blink, his eyes were agonisingly desiccated. Instinctively, he closed his dried eyes and waited for the explosion. It never came... Cautiously, he opened his eyes to find a blinding light. He then woke up...

Shelby Kurucz (13)
All Saints Catholic College, Dukinfield

Distorted Reality

I sprinted towards the bunker, breathless. The secure cave opened with ease. Reluctantly, I entered. It shut tight as I entered the threshold. Simultaneously, the lights flickered on revealing the mass destruction that had occurred. I heard screams and squeals. I approached the door, shaking. The screams fell silent, I peered out of the door. My pupils dilated. Suddenly, an army of malicious machines appeared. They marched in absolute synchronisation with one aim, to eliminate all humans. They cascaded through the door and pounced. I had no chance. But if this happened, would I be here to tell the tale?

Brandon Whendero (13)
All Saints Catholic College, Dukinfield

Pandemonium, Can We Stop It?

The beginning of the end, that's how they described it. Death, pain, destruction. What else can I say? Thousands of cataclysmic events collide within me. Spine-chillingly motivated by the screams on the outside. I feel alone, I am alone. Examining my surroundings, trepidation conquers my body. My nightmare has appeared, and there is nothing I can do about it. Fearfully, the screams outside fall silent, making my whole body freeze. Endless questions fill my head, I have no idea what just happened. Or if it may happen again. I hear a loud shriek, but it isn't a person. I'm next...

Jessica Mason (12)
All Saints Catholic College, Dukinfield

Supernatural War

A bright light burst from the horizon. The machines marched, the war had begun. Fighting against us because they didn't understand us. The government had tried to keep witches hidden. They had brought bright torches. Sprinting towards the bunker, I was too afraid to keep fighting. I was aghast at what was happening. Screams began to ring throughout the battlefield. My mother held me close, hoping that we would survive the witches. The screams outside fell silent. I found so many burnt bodies. A misshapen figure pulled on my arm. I disappeared. Gone! But where? I didn't have a clue.

Elena Mayes (14)
All Saints Catholic College, Dukinfield

Historic Bomb Attack

The machines marched, the war had begun. They marched their way to the front, gathered around and stared. Emotions filled the air as the bright blue sky flipped. Smoke gathered the air as the horrid monsters charged with no fear. Black metal swords clashed with one another, less fell to the ground. The life-threatening bombs exploded like balloons popping. Only had a few dark soldiers left fighting on their behalf. Darkness filled the air as all soldiers fell like heavy bricks to the ground. Red velvet blood everywhere as the fighters had a disturbing end to their final exotic mission.

Lydia Wheeler (12)
All Saints Catholic College, Dukinfield

Robots

The smoke cleared. I wasn't prepared for what I was about to encounter. Embers covering the floor like a thick blanket. Footprints illustrated across the floor with each individual pattern, like a snowflake. This all began with the lack of aspiration in my small town. Robots scuttered all around town. Demolishing anything in their path, fireballs roaring, children screaming. Mayhem struck the lifeless town. I hid far below the ground. The screeches of children giving me a headache, I tried to block it out but I knew that destruction won and I no longer had my family or my home.

Isabelle Proffitt (13)
All Saints Catholic College, Dukinfield

The Secret War

Bang! A cloud of wispy smoke viciously engulfed me, choking me. Bullets sped rapidly, narrowly missing me. The opposition was nearing victory. A storm of soldiers patrolled past me triumphantly as I lay down silently. Now, it was the wind's turn to look down and push me as gunshots fired. I had an advantage, I hurriedly paced towards a huge, grey, concrete block and ran inside. I was greeted by a long, thin hallway with a red velvet carpet, a hazelnut-brown door for every room, encrusted with diamond doorknobs. I opened a door to see its deepest, darkest secrets...

Finlay Jake Hughes (13)
All Saints Catholic College, Dukinfield

The Cataclysmic, Chaotic Incident

We were the only ones left, the disease had spread like wildfire. We had no idea how this had all started, no idea about what happened to those we loved. Everything became dejected and despondent, nothing mattered. Everyone was afraid of death, even more from when there was no disease. The world became pessimistic hastily, it was as though everything had abruptly shut down. This happening never made anyone judge their life as much as this, everyone felt as though they should have done more. More fun, more happiness, more great things to remember. Was this the beginning or end?

Chloe McCue (14)
All Saints Catholic College, Dukinfield

Fear

We were the only ones left, yet a troubled presence filled the atmosphere, choking us, filling our lungs with emptiness. But there was no sound. Silence spread through the air like a contagious disease in a room full of people. Nobody spoke in fear that we weren't alone. We feared that something was watching us. Watching our every move, stalking us. We felt it. Watching from the shadows, waiting. We carried on, making sure not to make a sound. Our fear controlled us throughout our lives. That's what was watching, our deepest, darkest fears. We were the only ones left.

Amelia Sweeney (14)
All Saints Catholic College, Dukinfield

Revolution

The smoke cleared! We weren't prepared to face the revolution. As the gloomy, grey smoke started to clear, I could see the desolate city surrounding me. It was empty, plain. It felt deserted like it'd been empty for thousands of years. As I stared around, I started to notice that this was the world that I'd always 'lived' in, the place I called home, where I'd grown to be the person I am. Where 'they' decided who should live and who should die. Where 'they' decided who should be miserable and who should be happy. Would today be my day?

Olivia Palma-Neal (14)
All Saints Catholic College, Dukinfield

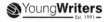
Alone

Sprinting towards the bunker, I heard noises. But these weren't anything human, nor animal, no, it was like Death itself. Although I didn't believe in ghosts, this made me slightly doubt my beliefs. Also, I was alone in this forbidden world, at least I thought. I was alone because on July 3rd there was a strange smell and I entered this alternate universe. Yes, I wanted to be alone. No. Not like this. Anyway, these noises were strange, they were... memorable. Everything around me started spinning, I saw my memories.
Suddenly, I woke up in a white room, alone...

Shannon Williams (13)
All Saints Catholic College, Dukinfield

The End

I sprinted towards the bunker, it was locked. The war had begun. I wasn't safe. I had to find a way to get inside the bunker. Everything was chaotic, sounds of children and women screaming filled the air. Shots were being fired, the machines marched on, killing and destroying. Not one living thing was left alive. The army of destruction had left. I was still hidden, too terrified to move. The smoke in the air was clearing swiftly. It was dark. I got up. Sweat trickled down my face. All my childhood memories were fading, my village was destroyed.
"Nooooo!"

Muhammad Hasan Masood (13)
All Saints Catholic College, Dukinfield

Highest Place

My childhood was great, I had friends and a supportive family, I loved life. Until high school came. Juice turned into alcohol, lollipops turned into cigarettes and the only drug I used to know was cough medicine. My friends started dropping out of school because they were too busy getting high. They had their heads in too deep, too deep that they didn't want reality anymore. There were groups of people that went into shops and stole food and drinks because the money they had was 'drug money'. Soon, small crimes turned into murder. Everybody who lived here left.

Ellica Fryer (14)
All Saints Catholic College, Dukinfield

The Beginning Of A New Era

The machines marched, the war had begun. Stood waiting for the command, all I could do was wish my family were still alive. Mankind was no longer superior. Intellectual robots outsmarted the creators and as a consequence, we now had to fight for our power. The word 'attack' bellowed throughout the rundown trench. Guns clicked in slow motion. Screaming voices alarmed everyone. This wasn't supposed to happen to me. Maybe if I left now, I could survive, make my own home away from this chaotic abyss. I stood to run but then a sharp pain went through my chest...

Maya Patel (12)
All Saints Catholic College, Dukinfield

Hope In Hell

The screams outside fell silent as Hope entered the forest. Knowing she needed to find food, she walked on. Atlanta had been bombed, spreading a disease that made the dead walk the Earth, killing people as they went. She had fought through, this was because her dad had trained her for this. The 'things' were attracted to sound so she laid low. A place named Terminous was offering sanctuary for all so that's where she was heading. After a very long night, Hope headed to the sanctuary. Sadly, there wasn't one. She was killed like cattle, her throat slit.

Emma Atkinson (12)
All Saints Catholic College, Dukinfield

Hurricane

The smoke cleared! We weren't prepared for what was about to happen. My heart racing, my legs shaking. "Follow me," I whispered to her.
After the huge hurricane, we walked to the old, frightening but well standing tree. We were very curious and confused about why it was only these three things left. We could see all the roofs being blown off houses and random leaves and branches that fell off trees. I was petrified and didn't have a clue what I was supposed to do. It became silent. Suddenly, I heard a squeak, it sounded like a haunted mouse...

Amelia Walczyk (13)
All Saints Catholic College, Dukinfield

Empty World

The screams outside fell silent, the wind itself stilled. The remaining people wept for the unlawful deaths caused by the constant havoc we had been living in. Seven other mayhem-driven people survived, we were disordered, confused and riotous, everyone was looking out for themselves. All the comfort we were deprived of dispersed into the air and flew away with the wind. Our souls begged for peace but our hearts longed for freedom. Before the war broke out, most people my age longed for death but now the Grim Reaper was knocking on our doors. We hid and ran away.

Lily Cotterill
All Saints Catholic College, Dukinfield

Chaos

A bright light burst from the horizon, I was terrified and trying to protect my family that were left with me. Soldiers came marching from the distance over the huge hill. Swiftly, all of my teammates pulled out their weapons and sprinted towards them, another huge explosion puffed the sky with pitch-black smoke, killing the innocent people around. Suddenly, the whole Earth turned silent. I was crouched with my hands over my ears. War had come to an end. Millions of bodies and injured people lay dead on the rock-solid concrete in pain. This was the official end.

Aimee Lauren Scholefield (13)
All Saints Catholic College, Dukinfield

Uncontrollable

The screams outside fell silent, that was the moment I knew everything was a catastrophe. There was something out there, something malicious. I swallowed my breath with fear, with terror and chaos, in case I made the slightest noise and it found me. It was terrifying, was I the last one left? Had I survived and no one else had? The curiosity was running across my spine in agony. Everything swarmed around me. There were noises, my skin rattled with apprehension. I was troubled, it was getting closer and closer. I shivered in the silence, then the pain was gone.

Chillie Allen (12)
All Saints Catholic College, Dukinfield

The Bunker

I sprinted towards the bunker, the horrifying screams made me hesitate... I started to think it was my destiny to save them. I stopped, I heard my mum scream and she started to cry. I turned around, she was lying there with her arms and legs missing. I dropped to my knees, my eyes started to water... She looked at me and said, "Don't be afraid, it will be okay."
I got up and ran as the things roamed around the city streets, searching for any unlucky people. I was terrified but then the sound stopped.
"Are they still there?"

Kie-John William Booth (13)
All Saints Catholic College, Dukinfield

The Silence

The screams outside fell silent. We were the only ones left. Still, I could hear ammo rounds ringing in my ears. Once I was sure the building was clear, I stood up. Silently, I looked out of the windows. You could still see the green-snake gang leaving. I felt salty tears slide down my face. *What has the world become?* Gangs controlled everywhere, the population had dramatically decreased and areas were uninhabitable. Not to mention polluted. Quickly, I wiped away my tears whilst I thought of my old home. It was the first city to fall in the war...

Mya Irvine (13)
All Saints Catholic College, Dukinfield

What It Takes To Survive

I sprinted towards the shelter. With the growing amount of walkers outside, I had to think fast. When I registered that I was alive, I realised I had no weapons or supplies. Right there, on the table, was a hammer, it wasn't much but it could certainly bash their brains out.

"Always in the head," James had said.

I missed James. After all, he was the one who had taught me how to survive the zombie apocalypse. After a few minutes of pondering, I found some food and water under a wooden plank.

"Still not bitten..."

Dylan Catlow (12)
All Saints Catholic College, Dukinfield

We Need Change

A great war was started by those who called us terrorists. Famine was wiping out most, besides the few who had more than enough. Downhearted, people turned to the only people who had the courage to get what they wanted. Gangs gave the depressed population hope of survival. We had control. The machines marched, the war had begun to get much worse for the rich but much better for the gangs. Marching in pride, we went through panic-ridden communities where most were dead, injured or too aghast to move from their bunkers. This was the beginning of the end.

Emily Phillips (13)
All Saints Catholic College, Dukinfield

Nothing Left

The screams outside fell silent, I knew I was now alone. I'd always heard tales of the last human on Earth but never did it cross my mind that the last person would be me. Cautiously, I ventured from my capsule into the burning city. Orange and crimson hues danced a ritual in the streets, smearing distress across my face. Smoke swallowed me, haunting my every move like a sinister spirit in the midst of the abnormality. I gulped: was I responsible now? Did the entirety of the human race lean on my shoulders? Self-deprecation kicked in, was I enough?

Tia Anthony (13)
All Saints Catholic College, Dukinfield

Darkness And The Bombs

Me and my friends sprinted to the bunker whilst bombs dropped all around us. Trampling, we ran, pushing and shoving, trying to get safe no matter the cost. Then it hit. "Help!"

Boom! Silence flooded the grounds. Timmy was dead. Darkness surrounded the field. All I could see was crimson blood flowing over his body. I didn't know what to do. I had been scarred for life with no way to forget about it. I ran. I ran as far as I could. Screams faded and anger took over my body. This was my end, the bombs were coming, goodbye!

Joseph Jordan Ettore Ardolino Lee (11)
All Saints Catholic College, Dukinfield

The Local Trauma

We were the only ones left. The town had been captured by the criminals. Hearts pounding, lights flashing, we knew that they were the wanted teenagers that had been causing the local trauma. A cluster of boys rolled up in black cars and suddenly, the teenagers scarpered. Shortly after this unfortunate meeting, there was a new update on the news that riots had been triggered. We knew who was to blame for this despicable behaviour. We all met up and headed to the centre of town. All we could see were police cars and a variety of people scattered...

Jasmine Hughes (13)
All Saints Catholic College, Dukinfield

The War Had Begun

The machines marched, the war had begun...
Slaughter, chaos, murder. The innocence of the
village dropped like flies, like moths to a flame as
the evil lured them in. Blood and anguish clogged
the air, suffocated the men, women and children
as they took their last breath. All gone... Not a man
in sight, not even a bee to buzz through the air.
Everything fell to silence. A deep emptiness
hovered like a blanket over what took place before
the very eyes of the waking moon. Nothing but
barren land. The machines chugged to a stop.
Their job was done.

Molly Phillips (15)
All Saints Catholic College, Dukinfield

The Old Lady

As I was standing outside the petrifying, old palace, I noticed that the windows were cracked, the light was blinking and the giant spider was walking. There was a graveyard outside the palace with an old lady standing there. She was wearing all white, she had black hair and her face was all burnt... She was holding a candle in her hand. She was holding her eye in the other. She turned her neck around all the way. She started to laugh really loudly and suddenly, bright lightning came down. Panicking, I woke up and realised I was just dreaming.

Ayesha Asjad (13)
All Saints Catholic College, Dukinfield

Gone

The screams outside fell silent as I quickly slammed the heavy metal door, isolating me from the public. As I dashed around the building, looking for life, I noticed a small window in the distance, giving me a view of the outside. Gone. The roads, buildings, civilisation, it was all gone. The wave from the clashing, dark blue sea ended all human life here. I was heartbroken. The last thing I saw before I swung the door shut was a monstrous 54-foot wave, hovering above the overly-crowded city. My heart began to crumble and ache. Sadly, gone.

Casey-Joyce Wilson (13)
All Saints Catholic College, Dukinfield

Sweet Like Honey

"Follow me," it whispered. It was a little suspicious but anywhere was safer than here. Anywhere at all. I ran after it, running through the bare streets with lifeless bodies everywhere. I swallowed a lump in my throat as I saw the people closest to me, pale and thin. The 'thing' took me to what once was a forest and took some sap off a tree, handing it to me. I thanked the odd creature and swallowed it, the first food I'd had in months. It was sweet, almost like honey. I liked sap. I could die from its sweetness...

Summiyah Khalid Nazir (14)
All Saints Catholic College, Dukinfield

Apocalypse

We were the only ones left... people that is, it had been two days since the zombie apocalypse started, chemicals were in the air, food couldn't be grown and we were starving. There wasn't much time, we had to go to the shelter... Would we make it alive? So far, the zombies had taken over all of the city. They'd taken over all of the buildings. As we were walking through a forbidden part of the forest, we heard rustling in the bushes and breeze. We saw a note on the ground saying: 'No further!' But we took a step...

Lacey Irvine (11)
All Saints Catholic College, Dukinfield

Not Afraid

We were the only ones left. As I stumbled through the deserted bunker, I opened the dusty, decayed door and there were houses in flames, windows shattered, cars breathing out flames. An enormous truck exploded in the distance, my vision went blurry. There was a dreadful ringing in my ears. I slammed the door shut. I couldn't hear or see anything. *Bang!* There was an incredibly frightening noise at the door.

"Let the games begin," the noise refrained.

I had to play 'the game'. I had to survive...

Aisha Hussain (13)
All Saints Catholic College, Dukinfield

The Smoke Changed Everything

Walking down the blossom street, it was such a beautiful day. Roses blooming, crystal-blue sky, not one cloud in sight, the shimmering sun shone against the town. But then everything changed, the sun went down, dark black clouds covered the whole town, plants died. People started running around, confused. It was chaos. It was like a lunar eclipse but worse. Suddenly, thick smoke pounced on us. I ran for my life, it was so fast but I made it to this building. I felt my body shake. But I wasn't prepared for what was to come next...

Kelsey Burlingham (14)
All Saints Catholic College, Dukinfield

The Unknown Beast

A bright, luminous light shot up from the horizon. Jaws dropped left, right and centre, I gazed in the distance! What was it? How had it happened? Could we all be dead in just a matter of time? Panic-stricken, me and the many people in the town ran for our dear lives. Emerging over the mountains, a menacing-looking, exotic, colossal bull headed our way. I was shaking. Scrambling for cover, I ran like a cheetah hunting for its prey. When I arrived at the destination, a shiver ran up my spine. It wasn't enough, I was now a victim.

Finlay Bland (13)
All Saints Catholic College, Dukinfield

Bleeding Scream

I thought the world was our home, a society of people who were inspired by others. No. As the bombs started exploding and the guns started shooting, I couldn't do anything. Time was ticking. The world was coming to an end, World War III had just begun. A light burst from the sky, blinding everyone with its brightness. A bleeding scream. Too shocked to start fighting, people realised we needed to save the world but it was too late. The world was over but until this day, no one would know who screamed blood until Friday the 13th.

Katie-Jay Starowojtow (12)
All Saints Catholic College, Dukinfield

The Beginning Of A New End

As he sprinted towards the bunker, the war machine fired flaming, fast bullets, they patted on the side of his head. Smashing his head on the bunker floor, he was shocked to see all of the dead bodies piled upon the floor in the distance. He took a glimpse of a minuscule child crying in the corner. Suddenly, the boy was dragged away. This was how he knew he had been set up... A tall-looking creature crept out of the dark corner, the boy's torso dangling from his mouth. He took a gulp and thought, *it's all over now.*

Owen Gee (13)
All Saints Catholic College, Dukinfield

The Cry For Help...

The machines marched, the war had begun... Alarms of cars were going off, smashing of windows and screams of innocent people. People's lives were at stake and nobody could stop it. *Bang!* Suddenly, the screams stopped, bombs exploded, the world fell to pieces as the lives of others stopped in a heartbeat. Hearts shattered and the cries of civilians broke out for help. Desperately, everyone searched for a way out over and over again but there was no luck. I could see the desperation in their innocent, pure, loving eyes.

Megan Leigh Neeson-Taylor (12)
All Saints Catholic College, Dukinfield

The Dead Alive

It was a chemical riot. The end of the world, we thought. It was the year 9000, it was my birthday, you see I was throwing a huge party. My father was downstairs performing his science projects. All of a sudden, there was a *crash!* My father ran upstairs and launched me an oxidation mask and told me I had to evacuate. It turned out he smashed a miniature container full of zombie antidote which could affect a country. We didn't have enough money to leave so we waited in his top-secret bunker and waited for a survivor.

Curtis Hall (13)
All Saints Catholic College, Dukinfield

The Super-Duper Death Story

I sprinted towards the bunker. The zombie-looking creatures chased after us. The screams outside fell silent. People dropping like flies. Just like that, half of the human race wiped out faster than you could even blink. We were the only hope left for the sake of the human race. This new gloomy world began no longer than 24 hours ago. The only thing I remember is the rush hour. Cars crashing, turning and exploding, trying to get away from these zombie-like creatures. Was this the end of the world we knew and loved, or a new one?

Bailey Dean (13)
All Saints Catholic College, Dukinfield

The Dark Whispers

Whispers trying to draw me into the darkness, I would never go near it. The golden, shimmering sun went away and darkness had come. I tried to sleep but the fear of them finding me and ferociously penetrating my head kept me awake. Waking later with my bladder about to burst, I needed the toilet. I crept out of the car and to a tree that was in the forest, there I delightfully let it out. Pulling up my pants, I heard what sounded like saliva drip on the floor. Looking behind, it sat there, looking evil, staring at me...

Anisha Saxon (13)
All Saints Catholic College, Dukinfield

Chaos

The screams outside fell silent, all the screaming, crying, gone. It was peaceful. As I cautiously walked out of the bunker, I was dreading what was ahead of me. The bitter breeze hit me as I walked out onto the street and memories swarmed around me; the buildings where I grew up, half-destroyed. Bodies filled the streets. I was alone. Not knowing what to do next, I panicked, all that was on my mind was my family and friends. What was I supposed to do now? I said to myself, "What has the next generation come to?"

Katie May Summer Wyatt (14)
All Saints Catholic College, Dukinfield

The Cruise Of The Jungle Monster!

I sprinted towards the bunker like I was running a marathon. Running to save my life, I didn't think I would make it. "I need to hurry," I said to myself as I thought I was going to be eaten.

Running through the trees was like running from a wild dog. I could see the bunker in sight and cheered with joy but then realised I needed to start running, making it through the door was like running to your parents after being away for a long time. I climbed into bed and hid so the monster couldn't find me!

Preston Warren Hiorns (13)

All Saints Catholic College, Dukinfield

Industrial Revolution

The machines marched, the war had begun. We were the only ones left, we had to do something. We peered out of the bunker hatch and could see only smoke and vapour and titanic machines searching for survivors on the ground. Suddenly, its robotic neck twisted to face our bunker, we heard a loud bang on the hatch and then silence... The machines had lost interest and moved on. Me and the others peered out one more time and I stepped outside. The wind felt nice and cool. We began to run and run, not knowing when to stop...

Joe Stott (13)
All Saints Catholic College, Dukinfield

The Riot

I sprinted towards the bunker, scared. I was falling while the riot was happening. It was the scariest night of my life. The riot felt like a war. There were gunshots. There were dead bodies everywhere on the floor. It was like a bloodbath on the streets. I was inside the bunker, looking through the holes. It was like WWII all over again. There was a killer on the loose and that killer was near the bunker that I was in. The person was a killer and he was wanted. He was chasing me with a machete. "Arghhhhh!"

Ermal Brahimi (12)
All Saints Catholic College, Dukinfield

All We Felt Was Despair

We were the only ones left. The war outside failed to surprise us by now. We all lost control, betrayed and empty, that was all we felt. We were helpless, our powers were too weak to face the out-of-control world. So many of us felt despair, life had no hope... Hope... the world still made me bitter. We all had it but he took it away from us, but mostly gave us despair. We all turned aggressive, annoyed and jealous of our former family. I couldn't believe what it had come to. Despair had won, we were hopeless.

Emily Dixon (12)
All Saints Catholic College, Dukinfield

Everything In Nothing

The night went silent. Everything stopped. It seemed that the world had frozen, life was empty, the air still. I couldn't scream for help. I was helpless. There wasn't a thing I could do but stand in the cold night. Everyone was watching me but I was alone, always alone. I wanted to be safe in my own home, but there I was in the middle of the Earth, worrying about nothing. I couldn't handle it. All I wanted it to be was how it used to be. I finally had hope. It came so quickly. My scream took over.

Madison Douglas (12)
All Saints Catholic College, Dukinfield

The Eruption

In the dead of night, everything was tranquil. Nothing ringing in my ears. No people running around insanely. But little did I know, this was about to change. Except that I was alone. Suddenly, a bright light burst on the horizon and the area erupted in chaos. A large, quite scary man burst into my room. As he was dragging me to safety, I came to a realisation: a realisation that this was the end! I had to escape the madness. So I ran. Jumping over heaps of bodies, it came to me. I was the only one left alive.

Amelia Mae Brunt (13)
All Saints Catholic College, Dukinfield

The Explosion

A vivid light glistened from the horizon, the flashlight shone into my eyes as I held my hands up saying, "I'm not one of them."
I looked around and they were all gone. I was devastated, wondering how one chemical explosion could cause so much devastation! It all started when a group of scientists were trying to make a cure for a new disease, when it all exploded. Everyone went crazy and started to riot like a heap of monkeys. I was overwhelmed with guilt, as I, was one of the scientists.

Kelsey Buxton (13)
All Saints Catholic College, Dukinfield

Faded Away

We were the only ones left... The war was brutal. Forsaken on a dull, futile planet. The blaring alarm eerily came to an immediate halt. There was complete silence. I could hear my stomach churning. A cloud of smoke filled the air. I saw two famished figures. I peered at their shadows. They were shady and unfamiliar. They had clothes as dark as the night sky. I felt cold shivers down my spine. I finally stepped out. The people faded into nothing. I felt a bullet pierce through my skin. Humanity was extinct.

Esha Zaffar (12)
All Saints Catholic College, Dukinfield

The Deathtrap

I sprinted towards my bunker as quick as a flash. We were sprinting for our lives as the German planes flew over the bunker. I shut the door and prepared to set foot in a less chaotic area. Suddenly, there was a bang, a gush of smoke was in the bunker and then I collapsed, not remembering anything.

I woke up next to a broken tree. Then a voice called, saying, "Come home."

It got louder and louder until we got there, we realised we were in a deathtrap and then we knew it was a deathtrap.

Thomas Apruzzese (12)
All Saints Catholic College, Dukinfield

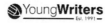
The Trafford Centre Scare

It was mid-afternoon and people were splashing their cash until the unexpected happened. The Trafford Centre was still jam-packed with people and from the top floor was a deafening scream. I ran up to see what it was and it was horrifying. Someone had been shot in the head. I knew what this meant. It meant there was a killer in the Trafford Centre. I quickly shouted, "There's a killer! Run!" at the top of my voice.

It was too late, the killer had locked all of the doors. It was over!

K Brierley (12)
All Saints Catholic College, Dukinfield

The Last Of Us

We were the only ones left. It was very silent, no noise at all. It was a weird feeling being out here all on my own with no one beside me. It only felt like five minutes ago the world was normal but maybe for others, it didn't. Being all alone out here wasn't fun since everyone had mysteriously disappeared. As I walked on the grey, broken pieces of glass below me, I feared that something would soon come towards me, catch me by surprise. Scared as I was, I picked up my bat and put it near me...

Kirsty McCue (12)
All Saints Catholic College, Dukinfield

The Toxic Acids

As I woke up thinking that it would be a normal, boring day I found it was the complete opposite. The blood-red sky surrounded the area we were in and the loud screams filled the air which seemed to last forever. I got out of my bed, walked out of my house... Fire, blood and chopped off heads were squished and exploded all over the floor. There was a strong smell of toxic chemicals on the floor, about to explode and destroy everything. But then I jumped and woke up with a massive headache that killed!

Jessica Mary Thompson (12)
All Saints Catholic College, Dukinfield

The End Of Eternity

Wow, this is the world we live in, I thought. I was so sad, I felt dead. There was no one around me. Who knew that global warming could do this to us? The world I knew was beautiful and colourful and had life everywhere you went. But now, it all looked dead and dull. How did this happen? I thought, *all these beautiful flowers I planted in my backyard are dead and dry, there is no life around me.* I never knew I would be the last person. This was the end, the Earth was finally gone.

Amie Mbye (13)
All Saints Catholic College, Dukinfield

Burning Horizons

A bright light burst from the horizon. Me and my crew raced and we went through the forest which was set on fire. We could see the bunker, when we got to it the fire was getting closer and closer! I counted my crew and we were one short. He was outside. I screamed to him, all I could hear was him screaming in pain. We were all scared and the cabin shook like a hurricane. It was abominable. We shook more and we flew into the air into the fire and we violently skidded into the spiky, burning tree!

Paige McNally (12)
All Saints Catholic College, Dukinfield

What's In The Bunker?

I sprinted towards the bunker, what was inside the bunker? Were there any traps? Would something eat me while I was sleeping? I thought that I was done for and I thought I'd be destroyed if I opened that door. Anyway, I was confident that nothing was in there, but I was wrong. I set foot in the bunker and guess what happened? I stepped on a trap. Vines wrapped around my legs and arms. I saw a sword so I grabbed the sword and cut the vines. The vines went back into the hole. Yay! I escaped.

Jasmine Davenport (12)
All Saints Catholic College, Dukinfield

Our World

It was bright and early in the morning. I took one little look out of the window, all I could see were big grey clouds caused from all the gas and oil that came out of the car exhausts. The thought of what the Earth used to be and what it was now made me sick. It was getting out of hand, it wouldn't only cause global warming, it could cause mayhem on the roads, people raging due to the climate change. Soon there would be nothing left on Earth and it was all our fault. We needed to change.

Amy Bailey (13)
All Saints Catholic College, Dukinfield

Follow Me

I sprinted towards the bunker and my heart was thudding. *Boom! Boom!* I could hear voices all around me. My head was a mess, like a whirlpool of emotions. A creature was following me. Or was it? Suddenly, from in front of me, I heard a voice. "Follow me," it whispered from around the bunker. A pin dropped behind me, there was a shriek from behind the bunker door. I stopped running and stood, frozen to the spot. At that moment, I realised it was only a nightmare...

Isabella Mansell (13)
All Saints Catholic College, Dukinfield

Oblivion

The smoke cleared, we weren't prepared. As the bombing noises started to fade away, fear ran through my veins as my bony hands which were pointed towards the towering trees started trembling in fear. *Did it work?* I thought as I widened my eyes in wonder. I slowly moved my head around, observing millions of dead bodies lying on the sandy floor which was covered in blood. The dark, gloomy field was as quiet as a graveyard and you could hear a pin drop... This was oblivion.

Ellaine Wahome (13)

All Saints Catholic College, Dukinfield

Escape

As I sprinted faster than a lightning bolt towards the bunker, my heart was racing. Gunshots! We were the only ones left. Fear was overtaking my body, it was over but I had to try and survive, if only for a short time. I knew I had to try and save the world! But we couldn't do it alone. But at that very moment, a scream... It was our general. His arm flew into the air. We were friends. A tear trickled down my face. We shot our last bullets, it was over. Or was it? *Bang!*

Ronnie Pelech (12)
All Saints Catholic College, Dukinfield

Ending The Cause

I can't remember what exactly happened, only a flash... Then the sky fell. Everyone was gone. I remember cowering in a WWV bunker with my siblings and twenty-ish others. When we left, everything was in ruins. Gone. Like they'd never been there. My brother suggested it first. He said to 'do something'.

I replied, saying, "What? Go all edgy and become warlords? Like everyone does in apocalypse movies?"

I was being sarcastic, but all he said was yes. That's how we're here today. Lord Kaos' top assassins. He was the one who caused this, now I'm gonna end it...

Georgia Nelson
Fazakerley High School, Aintree

Bye

"Follow me," a voice whispered.

I looked around the deserted space. Nothing was there. I crept around the corner. A tall, dark, stick-like figure was mumbling.

"We're not safe, follow me."

I slowly walked up to it. All of a sudden, five alien-like creatures circled me. Was this the end? I squinted my eyes as I was startled. I held tightly onto my necklace and hoped I'd be okay. I couldn't die! I was the last person on Earth, I couldn't be the reason the population died this early. I had years left. At least, that was what I hoped...

Shannon Elizabeth Hamilton (13)
Fazakerley High School, Aintree

The Great Flood

A burst of blue rose from the horizon. People were screaming. "Flood!"

I looked at the news. "The polar ice caps have melted, global warming. We have sent this world doom! Water will flood every city so get to high ground. Quick!"

I darted to the top of the Empire State Building. The flood encased the whole city in ice-cold water. It has now been five years and New York looks like Atlantis. If you are wondering how I and 200 others survived, well let's just say we're not human anymore. We have adapted to our wet, challenging environment...

Chloe Jessica Hilton (13)

Fazakerley High School, Aintree

The Nuclear Ending

The word's out. It's the end of the world as we know it! The government planted nuclear bombs into the Earth's core 100 years ago and had permission to use them when the population was too big or because of the pollution. They decided to use them now! They've given each country a rocket that could hold 100 people at once. One was five minutes away from us. We got in the car and stormed to the rocket. There were too many people! *Boom!* The sound stormed through my ears, a nuclear bomb exploded. Oh no! I felt it...

Karim Sumanschi (12)
Fazakerley High School, Aintree

A Bright Light Burst From The Horizon

Did the sun just explode? A bright light burst from the horizon. Everyone screaming gave me a headache. Some people were pulling out their suntan chairs, thinking it was the hottest day of the year. It sure felt like it. Police were everywhere, telling everyone to stay inside and not come out. I saw an old lady, very confused, not knowing what was going on. So I went out to get her and there it was, the sky going yellow and orange rocks came shooting down, landing heavily on the floor, blocking my home entrance. Was it the end?

Brodie Elizabeth Gardiner (13)
Fazakerley High School, Aintree

The End Has Come

I was tested on. I was lied too. They said it wouldn't harm me but it did. It was time I got my revenge on them. When I went over to the pulsing, red button, I remembered all of it. It was terrible. I pressed it, the plan had begun. The clouds turned grey and hurricanes formed as I watched from above. *The end has come*, I thought. I watched as I saw the volcanoes erupt and tornadoes swirled. The virus had worked! I changed the weather. The Earth went dark but the weather continued on its path of destruction.

Harry James Williams (12)
Fazakerley High School, Aintree

Devastation

The screams outside fell silent, I looked out the window to see a dead body on the floor, they were still around after months. All I had to defend myself was a shovel covered in mud and blood. The streets were silent and deserted. It was scary to walk alone, just in case one of those horrible, messy zombies came after you. They had been around for ages and half of the Earth's population had gone. My mum, dad and my little sister got lost about a month ago and I haven't seen any of them since. It was devastating.

Emma Navin (13)
Fazakerley High School, Aintree

Falling Stars

A bright light burst from the horizon. The world fell silent. I squinted my eyes to catch a glimpse of what had just happened. I was not ready for what I saw, the sky was bright purple, blue and yellow. As angelic as it was, I felt a rush of fear. I suddenly realised the stars were falling. One by one. *Crash! Bang! Boom!* was all I heard, my ears were bleeding. I looked down to the breaking ground and saw hundreds of crushed bodies. A strange fear sensation rushed through my body, head to toe. Would I be next?

Ruby Cleaton (12)
Fazakerley High School, Aintree

The Rain

I sprinted towards the bunker... It was just me and my brother. Our parents were in another country. There was rain outside. It was infected. If you were touched by it, you would die. My mum and dad made a bunker for me and my brother in case of this event, it had many supplies. But this thing could happen forever. Four years later, we ran out of supplies and couldn't go out because we would die. What were we really going to do? We were isolated and we couldn't find out if our parents were still alive...

Michael Andrew Wright (13)
Fazakerley High School, Aintree

The End!

It's coming to an end. It's spread everywhere. What will we do? As the day turned into night, it was time to hide. It was time for everyone to go mad. I locked myself in a cupboard which no one could get into. I heard screaming. It had started. The drug, EAJ, had been let out, making everyone go mad. The only way you can survive is to eat human flesh. As I was sitting in the cupboard, a loud bang happened and the door started to creak. The door opened and a man stood there. Everything then went black.

Lucy Oates
Fazakerley High School, Aintree

The Abandoned

The clock struck four and the grey clouds looked to be hanging on a thin string. There was nobody in sight, even in the capital city. Just shop lights flickering. Why would some beast do that? A population of 15 billion humans and over 100 billion animals. There was no future for this planet, just 55,000 people mourning their loved ones. How could we cope? Being one of the only ones in their country, we had to unify. Rebuild our society. If there was any chance of survival, this was what we had to do.

Joseph Arands (13)
Fazakerley High School, Aintree

Darkness' Haven

A squelch came from above the roof. *Another one of those things*, I thought to myself. Ever since it happened, the sun made every animal into a gooey, fleshy mess. Nothing could escape it. Dogs? Melted. People? Melted. Fur? Melted. It was unstoppable. Unless you reached the 'site', most thought it was a myth, used by cannibals to lure prey. But now? I'm not so sure. Better to stay in my water tower for now, it keeps those things away anyway.

Thomas Wilson (12)
Fazakerley High School, Aintree

Panic. Fear. Hunger.

"Sapphire!" Henry shouted.

2050. The zombie apocalypse had struck. She was incredibly weak and fatigued. She was starving. Fighting for her life. Panic. Fear. Hunger. All pumped through her veins like blood. Trying to hold off the bloodthirsty, famished zombie that used to be her mother. The sun came shining down on the zombie, it disappeared.

"We should go to my crops," Henry suggested. They walked endlessly until they reached his desolate home. His crops were in ruins. Damaged. Destroyed. A lonely, wet tear dribbled down his fair, white skin. Sapphire was going to die...

"No!" Henry cried sadly.

Lucy Edwards (11)
Little Lever School, Little Lever

Rivers Of Blood

Bang! Bang! Bang! Bang! Bang! The screams outside fell silent. I was the only one left breathing. Bodies scattered all over, blood-covered bullets everywhere. I took a tentative step forward. I was in shock. There were corpses everywhere. *Drip-drop! Drip-drop!* Blood dripped all over the floor. They had gone. The vile people who did this were gone. I took two more vigilant steps forward. I was scared. Terrified. I heard voices. Quiet but deep voices.

"Over there!" I could hear.

They had all gone, or so I thought. *Bang! Bang!* I fell to the floor.

"Help me!"

Ella Morley (12)
Little Lever School, Little Lever

The End

Looking down through the darkness, I saw these weird-looking things, almost like zombies. As they made deafening noises, whilst hitting the dull bricks, it felt like a crazy dream. Confused, I stepped outside and zombies stood still, making ear-bleeding noises. Attacking me ferociously. Where was my family? The dead had awakened. I was forgotten and forbidden. Sprinting for real life, everybody was gone. Screaming for help, nobody was there. Searching the town, I realised this place was deserted. Crying all alone, I missed my family already. Why did I survive? Seconds later, an explosion happened. The world ended.

Zak Colman (11)
Little Lever School, Little Lever

The End That Never Ended

The machines marched. The war had begun! Fire and bombs had taken over our beloved planet. Nothing would be normal ever again! For twenty-four hours, seven days a week, nobody was safe. This was the alien invasion!
Only a couple of hours in, we were already losing. This was almost the end! Nobody had ever seen these mysterious but deadly creatures. Suddenly, everything changed. It sounded like an electric wave. Every single alien had fallen to the ground and slowly disappeared into thin air. Screaming and crying had gradually faded away as the planet discovered their victory. Aliens were defeated!

Eshaan Yaser (13)
Little Lever School, Little Lever

This Corrupt World

Stranded in the middle of the never-ending ocean, I watched atrocities unfold. My friends escaping this corrupt world. Whilst I waited to follow them, isolated and alone, I moved, avoiding the alien objects invading my home. Suddenly, I caught a glimpse of a shiny, white silhouette. Darting towards it, my instincts took over. My fin pushing all the contaminated water aside. I opened my mouth and ate the unknown object: tasteless and sharp, it tore my insides apart. Spluttering, I couldn't dislodge the foreign object from my blowhole. My life as a dolphin was finished, I escaped this corrupt world.

Keira Howard
Little Lever School, Little Lever

Risen From The Clouds

As the scaly, aggressive dragon rampaged forward, its devastating fire raided houses while smoke bellowed out from the others. Suddenly, light shattered through the murky clouds. Confusion reigned supreme. They stood and stared at the beautiful bright light, like it was a gift from God. It shone across the town. Everyone was waiting. Surprisingly, a man with a muscular body jumped out into the beast and hatched violently: blood and smoke erupted from the beast's severed neck. The dragon lay dead. Everyone was cheering with joy. Unexpectedly, the ground started to shake. He thought he had won...

Ruben Worthington (13)
Little Lever School, Little Lever

Unhappy World Of Haribos

Everyone knew there was something wrong. Helplessly they ran in fear, shouting and screaming. They were coming... The unicorns! They came from Planet Mars Bar in town, Hemia. They came with an army of killer gummy bears. One by one the unicorns stabbed the minuscule peasants with their horns. The gummy bears formed a sticky gummy goo into their delectable hands. Like a monstrous fireball, they threw the gummy goo directly targeting the innocent proletarians. Like superglue, the slimy goo stuck the minute people down to the ground so the unicorns could take their lives. All because of the Haribo...

Ellie Louise Steane (12)
Little Lever School, Little Lever

It Was A Pleasure To Burn

All of it was over, a mere and insignificant planet of inattentive monsters, once somewhat collected and carefree, now a broken one, submerged in melancholy, famine and malignant war. He stood in the middle of it all, watching billions of years of strenuous work and companionship become engulfed by omnipotent and malicious flames. Ash danced softly across his cheeks, bodies of the innocent surrounding his feet. He looked up, the serenity of the unilluminated sky causing a rush of amelioration to devour his very being. A wave of intuition washed over him. He felt relieved for the first time ever.

Maddison Dawson (12)
Little Lever School, Little Lever

Open The Door

The oaken door creaked open ominously. Curiously, the lead detective peered through the crack of the half-open door. It was dark. But the blinding light of the moon slowly began to envelop the room. Although only a slither of the room was visible, they could already see a blanket of crimson liquid, splattered violently across every corner of the room. With a large sigh, the lead detective finally opened the door fully, to be welcomed by piles of mutilated teens. Some were decapitated, some were disembowelled, they were all dead. All except one, whose scrawny body was trembling uncontrollably...

Nicole Lomas (12)
Little Lever School, Little Lever

The Day Things Changed Forever

Destructively, the navy sea crashed down the destroyed road, the skyscrapers gazed suspiciously down at the ground, glaring at the helpless people. Running for their lives, screaming and shouting, group by group they were abducted away by the strength of the Pacific Ocean. Buildings avalanched and crashed before their eyes as more and more buildings fell. A mother watched helplessly as her little girl was swirled away by the strength of the water, frantically shouting for help but nobody was there to help her: she took the decision to dive in after her. She quickly disappeared into the water...

Lexie Grant (12)
Little Lever School, Little Lever

Bots

A bright light burst from the horizon, it tore through the clouds, stripping it of darkness. The ground reverberated as the sea became a writhing, grey monster. Dwindling in the distance, three glistening blobs came to sight, three turned to ten and soon there were billions appearing. The smell of copper, iron and silver cluttered the air. The machine's eyes burned with simulated fury. It was clear, they only came to do one thing. Wind violently blew, causing trees to plummet to the ground, minimising any chance of survival. The robots drew closer and closer... Was this truly the end?

Lucy Jane Willett (12)
Little Lever School, Little Lever

Ammonia

The screeching outside fell mute as three boys woke up from their slumber. All of a sudden, the air felt... different. As if there was none. The boys went downstairs to find their mother lying lifeless on the floor, she was holding something. A letter. It read: 'The Himalayas'. Nobody understood. They agreed to go to the Himalayas. As they started climbing they found a small town. A sign read: *Hillfolk Town*. The boys started searching. They found people! They were alive! All of a sudden, a meteor crashed down. After all the smoke had cleared, they saw a girl...

Alyssa Hall (12)
Little Lever School, Little Lever

2075 London

It had been four months since the government had fallen. All sense of order and law had vanished. Crime rates went through the roof. There were drugs on every corner. Poverty flooded the streets, leaving a trail of pure devastation and misery behind. Not even a trace of the old life remained. Now, the streets were filled with the scents of the various drugs concealed within its pavements. That pulsed with the everlasting stench of nuclear warfare that would forever paint our streets red with the blood of our own suffering and honest deservingness for the sins we had committed.

Wahib Butt (13)
Little Lever School, Little Lever

The Resistance

Death, destruction, darkness. The year was 2050 and the world had succumbed to violence. But one ground hadn't, they kept fighting and they never gave up. One day, they saved a child. He never stopped trying to find them and after a year of looking, he found them. He fought with them. More people joined the fight. It wasn't enough, the resistance against war was falling quickly. But so was the violence. The world had been inspired by the resistance. The world stopped fighting because the resistance wanted a free world. Everyone stopped fighting and the war was no more.

Finley Schofield (12)
Little Lever School, Little Lever

Farewell My Friend

Melancholy, inky, gloomy, like a blanket suffocating us. The clouds intimidatingly watched and covered us. The wind was a beast, blowing chaos all around. Screams piercing our ears, only five of us made it.

"Which way shall we go?"

I could barely breathe, my heart pumping through my ribs.

"Help me!" Amy yelped as she got dragged away. The echo of her voice filled the air. We had to carry on running. I saw the bunker and ran in. The door slammed behind me... The group were trapped outside. The screaming went silent... Alone, I waited...

Olivia Vining (14)
Little Lever School, Little Lever

The End Is Near

Deadly, infecting Karar: the most lethal virus coming from a mad scientist and he put it in a crate full of money. Loading the crate into his plane, he zoomed into the sky. Opening the lid, he chucked it into an unprotected city. When the money landed, everyone gasped with excitement, running towards their death. Everyone, at least, got some and everyone ran to the shop ecstatically. But some people stopped, it was totally silent. People collapsed to the floor, holding their heads with rage and ran straight into the mob, angry with foaming mouths and murder in their eyes.

Lewis Martland (13)
Little Lever School, Little Lever

The Boy

A boy walked among a mass of straw hats and tattered cloth, the clatter of hooves and incoherent shouting engulfing his mind. He reached for his mother's hand, who aggressively grabbed ahold to keep her boy safe. Then it hit. A pulse of merciless strength rooted him to his position, like he had been cemented in time. His eyes darted to those other statues, emotion radiating from them without the need for words. Vivacious, black air stormed the crystal-blue sky, like a disease contaminating its host. Everyone ran, but not the boy. It threw him backwards. He had died.

Jack Ellis Walton (14)
Little Lever School, Little Lever

Screams In The Dark

The screams outside fell silent. The dark, misty landscape turned bright. The flashes of the artillery blinded anyone in its path. The heavy blanket of machine gunfire fell. Pain. Fire. Screams. Running out of the bunker, it hit, spreading its destruction left, right and centre. The machine guns marched, and the war had just begun. No-man's-land was scattered with the bodies of fallen comrades. Their last words crying out to their families, in hope everything would be okay. But it wouldn't. It was over. The light that once shone in their eyes died out for good.

Leah Lewis
Little Lever School, Little Lever

Cold War II

War, Russia, US. In the plains, people were living their lives. Russia was developing a new nuclear weapon, one was spotted. Two minutes from disaster. Russia had ordered a launch. Civil defence. Sirens failed. Smartphones warned to shelter from the fallout. Half of the Americans fell victim to the bomb. The survivors had an urge to kill. They turned to cannibalism. It was kill or be killed. The successful would face a tough nuclear winter. They had mutated and looked like they were from a horror or disaster movie. The Russians had won and the US was left devastated.

Harley Johnson
Little Lever School, Little Lever

The Silent Lands

The earth below my feet crumbles, releasing the cockroaches from its grasp. The silence stabs like needles, short-lasting, yet a pain that is never forgotten. This silence will likely continue on forever. The silence is ironically deafening, a sound that never ends. The silence is only created because of the existence of sound just like how darkness is created in the presence of light. The sound is gone completely from the world, for the simple reason that we are not worthy of it, the waves no longer crash since the sea had left with the sound. The silence remains.

Jacob Wiggins (14)
Little Lever School, Little Lever

A Traumatic Tuesday

As lightning struck over Amsterdam, Kieran awoke... startled. He ran downstairs, screeching, his face began to glow. It wasn't a normal glow, he began to glow redder by the minute, until his face was a tomato. A constant screech was heard in the dead middle of the night. Light after light flickered, door after door slammed. A man burst through the door, followed by some gruesome kids. All the lights went out, all the doors slammed, locking everyone inside. Suddenly, a bright light appeared from the horizon. All the doors opened and everyone ran, immediately...

Ellie Louise Mottershead (13)
Little Lever School, Little Lever

The Mother Of Dragons

I looked around me with elation. Fire engulfed the queen's colossal castle at Queen's Landing. My three children flew in the sky, burning the soldiers and the people. If not dead yet, they were suffering. My children's scales shimmered in the wind as they flew around in the night sky. Their leather wings glided as fire exploded out of their mouths. I walked through the fire as my soldiers held down the mad queen. The three dragons landed behind me as I walked down the Temple of Luna with my sword gripped in my hands, I swiftly decapitated the queen.

Michael Paul Bithell (12)
Little Lever School, Little Lever

Inevitable

"What a world we live in, violence, famine, crime. Across the planet we live in, chaos surrounds us. It has become a necessity for society to run properly. When did our planet become such a warzone? Was it 100 years ago in the beginning of WWI? Or after the September 11th attacks in New York?" asked the television presenter, as another shell hit the ground fifty yards away.

As the dust cleared, the sight of Anthony Baxter emerged from the wreckage. He opened fire across the town square, bodies dropped, last breaths drawn and chaos surrounded us.

Tom Hamlett (13)
Little Lever School, Little Lever

Subdued Reality

Glancing to my left and right, we all interlocked hands and took a step into the blazing sky. Slowly, I fell through the air, my life surrounding me. The floor continually neared us and as we sped up, we passed out. Subduing to reality, it made me realise in the final moments, that the difference between consciousness and unconsciousness was indistinguishable. The faster we plummeted to the ground, the more I felt my fear pulse through each and every vein, blood vessel and bone. As we came inches from the ground, light reached and then darkness, only darkness.

Kristian Taylor (14)
Little Lever School, Little Lever

The Apocalypse

I sprinted towards the bunker to get away from the zombies. All you could hear were the screams coming from outside the door. Then the screams fell silent, all you could hear was my heart racing like a cheetah. We were the only ones left, me and Ryan Collard-King.

"Follow me," I whispered, then through the window there was a bright burst from the horizon. Then I saw a shadow.

Ryan whispered, "Don't move, or they will see you and know that we are here."

We were forbidden from going out to the Dead Space or we would die...

Callum Murray (14)
Little Lever School, Little Lever

Cover Story

Everyone in our town was made by them to be the best. Every single feature genetically designed to be the best. Every house was the same height and width. Every family was the same size. Everyone eats, drinks and lives the same. But I'm different. I don't belong here. I sneaked in after the horrific war. I live with a genetically modified family. If I do anything wrong, they will know. Every day, it gets harder to lie to these innocent people. Now, people are getting suspicious about my cover story, I can't keep this a secret for much longer...

Sophia Magari (12)
Little Lever School, Little Lever

15 Minutes Of Silence!

Fifteen minutes had passed. Billions of people stood outside, in deafening silence. The core of society had gone. Electricity. No more social media. What were we supposed to do, talk? No one knew this would happen.

Twenty minutes had passed. Jaws slowly began to drop, as the taste of chaos sank in. People stepped out of their cars, screams sounded in every direction. Why did it happen? How did it happen? How could I reverse this? There must be a way that I could save society from this chaos. Could I be the hero that was remembered throughout history?

Caden Jones (14)
Little Lever School, Little Lever

The Deadly Dragon

A bulky, perilous, red dragon flew over the most enormous Viking city. The breath of a dragon is so poisonous that it could kill you in three seconds, or roast you where you stand. It was a hurricane, a tornado of death. Three days later, it was in Britain, blowing fire on buildings, vehicles and people. A large hurricane of fire smashed into the side of a building. Soon, the walls were crumbling down and people were falling out of the buildings and the dragon picked them up in his teeth and ate them.

"Yum! Yum!" the dragon roared loudly.

Sophie Martin (13)
Little Lever School, Little Lever

The Rising Undead

Clang! It was one o'clock and nearly time. I could feel my heart banging against my chest, about to burst through any second. The sweat trickled down my forehead, I waited stiffly. All of a sudden, I saw a wretched, scrawny, filthy hand rise from the ground. Rotten, stinking bodies emerged from the graves of Ravenswood graveyard. It was over: there were too many of them. Then they pounced... I drew my knife and slashed. One knocked me over from behind and I collapsed.
I woke up in what felt like a box, the lid was closed and locked...

Bethany Cain (12)
Little Lever School, Little Lever

Gang Warfare

"Help!" I shouted.

I went to my friend's house all the time but this was different. I'd been to my friend's house and I was nearly home. I was going down the back street, my house was just at the end.

"Arghhhhh!" I screamed as a gang of men jumped on me. Everything went black... my whole life flashed before my eyes.

I woke up, dead bodies all over the floor. I was really scared. There were men with guns everywhere. I took my last breath as the man pointed his gun at me. *Bang!* I fell to the floor.

Abby Gallagher (11)
Little Lever School, Little Lever

I Miss Them

We're the only ones left, me and my dog. The terrifying zombies are roaming the lands, killing everything in their path. Looking out of my bedroom, I see him. Six-foot tall, purple, my dog barks. He sees me. I run into my room, through the back door and within minutes, I am gone.
"Whoever finds the child and his dog will be freed from my army forever!" the ugly, purple man shouts.
Fear hits me. For once in my life, I miss my parents, they did everything for me. I miss them...
"Wake up." It was a dream all along.

Leon Jaydon Robert Tennant (12)
Little Lever School, Little Lever

Chaos Clashed With My Joyful Heart

The mystery smoke grabbed my face with anger, I was choking on my own useless breath. It started to clear: I could finally see something... A bright light burst from the slowly rising horizon, that was my expectation but in reality, it was a dead space that fell ghastly silent. Screams echoed into the distance, there lay my lifeless mum. Gone! I stood, paralysed in my own skin. Rivers of tears flooded down my sorrowful face into a puddle of depression. All the joyful memories were all deleted. Now, I'm wondering if that's what I deserve too.

Isla Marisa Jones (12)
Little Lever School, Little Lever

Chaos' Cold And Brief Dance

Solemn, stalking silence swept across the house as the darkness caressed the exterior of the building, seeping in through the window, seeking the light drawn to it like a starved wolf to its prey. The fresh scent of chemicals coming from down the hallway, the brisk smell of the crops wafted its way through the hall and up the nostril of any unsuspecting soul. The drought had left the moral on dregs like the wisps of a snuffed match. Gang wars and the screams of the family as the boss comes home drunken and violent, ready to lose almost everything.

Ellis Matthews (14)
Little Lever School, Little Lever

Isolated

I crawled closer to the gun, my leg throbbing, my sister spread across the field; dead. They edged closer, eyes fixed on the struggle in my face. "One pull of a trigger and it will all be over," I whispered.

They stepped closer. What were these vile creatures and what did they want? My stomach twisted and churned as I got a feeling that I was completely alone. Utterly alone. I gave up and spread across the field with my sister. A tear rolled down my cheek as I slowly slipped away. This was the end, these creatures had won.

Tilly-Anne Wilson (12)
Little Lever School, Little Lever

Voices

It was a dark night and the stars glistened in the sky. Heavy boots could be heard from an old warehouse, echoing through the sky. A young teenage girl was walking through a warehouse, looking for scraps. A sudden gush of wind flew and hit the girl, causing her cape to fly up and her hood to go down, revealing her black, faded into red, hair and her crimson-red eyes glistened in the light. "Go, get out, before it gets you," a sudden voice was heard, echoing through the walls of the warehouse.
"Be warned, go!"

Sarah Ashworth (12)
Little Lever School, Little Lever

Armageddon

I sprinted towards the evacuation site, I was safe at last. I heard the pleas of innocent people fade away as I stood there in my sorrow, planning on what to do next. The security didn't let me through because the ships were filled with women and children: the men were left to fight. As the smoke cleared, a monstrous, gruesome and blood-curdling beast leapt at men from the car debris. We were done for. There were no more living survivors left on the battlefield, only one was left, left to rot and die on the cold, dreaded battlefield.

Harry Owens
Little Lever School, Little Lever

Flames

I was running, running from the deadly, unstoppable flames that destroyed everything in their path. The flames chased me down into the destroyed nothingness, my bleeding heart was pounding with fear and terror and the mark of hope that was in me suddenly gone. I realised the deathly fact, my home was in a helpless and abandoned state, I was running again but this time I was running into the toxic and unknown darkness of the flames, the smoke surrounded me and I was blinded and choking, then I was awoken into a happy and amazing place...

Bettina Balic (14)
Little Lever School, Little Lever

Danger Destruction

Soon, there was destruction on Planet Earth. Where parts of the sun had struck the Earth like a lightning bolt. Making countries of the planet shatter and shake with earthquakes. The world of the human race was nearly extinct. Some survivors had found shelter. They were gathering supplies of food and enough water to keep them ready if everything vanished. The survivors had to reach the top of a mountain. The sun collided with the Earth and made the ice caps of the Arctic melt and flood all the islands. The sun had demolished the Earth.

Matthew Cowcill (14)
Little Lever School, Little Lever

The End

After the blast, there was nothing left, just ruins and the thick mist.

"Come here," a voice whispered from the fog, so I did, I followed.

The blanket of clouds blinded me, making it impossible to see what I was following. Suddenly, I was able to see, not a pretty sight, blood all over the walls. Then I realised I wasn't being helped. I was here to help end these savages' starvation. I felt an excruciating pain in my side, a weapon, I wasn't sure what it was but when it was pulled out, so was my life.

Louie Higgins
Little Lever School, Little Lever

A Silent Night

The silent night falls once again, the crackle of the fire burns through the whole city and the fear of not being able to defeat leaders of the revolution messes with someone's head every day. However, every day we lose a man every second to that fear where they can't stand being alive anymore. So they take their lives and take the easy way out. Now it is just me, no one left but me alone. My planet is about to fall through. Goodbye world, hope I did good for you. *Bang!* Then another silent night falls with no war.

Sophie Gorman (14)
Little Lever School, Little Lever

Mystery

My legs were trembling. My heart was pounding and I was breathless. I had been running for hours on end whilst trying to escape the mysterious beast chasing me and trying to engulf me with its bloodthirsty fangs. I didn't know what it was, I didn't know where it came from, but as soon as my eyes surveyed the strange creature I knew I had been running aimlessly deeper into the endless emerald forest. All I wanted was to escape from my wicked parents but I ended up in that situation. This is the story of how my life ended.

Charlotte Commons (12)
Little Lever School, Little Lever

The End Of Existence

As I ran into the bunker, the door slammed behind our sorrowful souls. Ten years later, the radiation started to affect us. So that night, we ventured out into the wilderness. As we walked, we found out that there was an antidote to this radiation. When we were 100 miles away from the antidote, we started to imagine, *what if it was a hoax or if the antidote was poison?* However, we carried on. Ten miles left. We spotted a colossal meteor so we ran the last ten miles. We arrived and shared the antidote, but it was a hoax.

Cameron Welsby (12)
Little Lever School, Little Lever

A Bad Dream

I sprinted towards the dark grey bunker and dived as a horde of flesh-eating zombies sprinted after me.

I woke up, checking for bite marks. Then I found it, a huge bite mark on my arm, blood everywhere. I ran to the bathroom to clean the wound. I was stood cleaning for a good twenty minutes when the light flickered. Then it completely turned off. Twenty minutes later, the light turned on and I looked up to see a tall man with long, bony fingers. Blood dripped from the jagged shard of glass. I turned to see no one...

Josh Taylor (13)
Little Lever School, Little Lever

Closing The Night

My heart pounded from running from weird creatures as chaos rained over my land, I thought I could beat it, but I failed. As darkness rained, I was crawling but I couldn't die at the moment, I had to survive the night as it was closing. All I had was a piece of metal to defend myself, I was plummeting down, staring at the night sky as I was eaten alive, the metal eroded from acid. My eyes dropped as I was already turning to something else and I wasn't ready to leave this world forever. Silence reigned, creepily...

Adam Marshall (14)
Little Lever School, Little Lever

Fire Creature

I ran out into the street filled with fiery flames. It was deserted, no one around except me. I walked down the abandoned street full of lifeless bodies. My heart pounding, remembering that the creature was still out there. I ran around, trying to find the creature. I heard a growling sound nearby. I looked over to see a zombie. It started to run towards me, I grabbed my pocketknife and ran towards the creature. I shoved my knife into its chest making it fall to the ground. I chopped its head off, it fell from the cliff.

Ashleigh Jade May (13)
Little Lever School, Little Lever

The Truth Of Number 10

Knowledge is power. Power is pride. Nothing says pride more than being Prime Minister. And so, I present to you, the truth of Number 10. In the depths of Downing Street and crevices of the Commons, lives a beast so feared that to some he is loved. Some say he was sent by the Russians in '52, others say he was once a man to which a terrible accident turned him to the left. That beast is the Jerimire Corybinite and if there is one thing that's clear, those who see him, freeze on their knees and tremble with fear.

Sam Percival (14)
Little Lever School, Little Lever

A Meteor From Outer Space

A meteor from another solar system hit Planet Earth. I was alone. Most of Earth had been destroyed but one city survived. That city was flattened. The skyscrapers were destroyed. The houses shredded apart. Somehow, I survived. No water, hardly any food and no electric. But I survived. Mum and Dad were at work and I just came home from school. I was home alone, I put on the TV and then the news. Apparently, a meteor was flying down to Earth. I remembered I had a basement to my house, I entered. I hoped I'd be safe.

Kaine Larkin (12)
Little Lever School, Little Lever

The Graveyard

The clock strikes twelve. I am walking my dogs around the village in the dead middle of the night, until I come to a church. I don't know what it is but my heart begins to beat a little faster. I begin to breathe heavier, my feet are perched on the ground, I cannot move. My dogs disappear, isolating me in the graveyard at the back of the church. Sweat trickles down my neck. The graves begin to rise. Before long, I am surrounded by these hideous creatures. I try to move, the terrifying beasts edge even closer...

Harley Irwin (13)
Little Lever School, Little Lever

Mission Apocalypse

I was trapped in the middle of the apocalypse. There were thousands of them, I swear. Maybe today was my last. I saw something running towards my area with a machete, I thought to myself that the creatures were getting stronger and smarter. I saw what it was, it was a human helping me. He could kill but why would he waste his time saving me? I hopped out of the car, helping the man who was defending me. After the crowd of creatures, there was silence. He then walked away, leaving me alone, stranded, with nothing.

Shane Naughton (14)
Little Lever School, Little Lever

Betrayed

I was a normal human once. Well, that was before they turned me into this. These unforgivable traitors that quivered beneath me, it was all their fault! They had revealed the hidden darkness deep within me. I refuse to tell you how. I was like a pawn on a chessboard that stayed in the same place. I was no human anymore; I was a monster biting my tongue, trying to hold back. But it didn't stop me. After the depression hit me, I finally left. They didn't know I had gone of course, but I would soon return...

Grace Harwood (12)
Little Lever School, Little Lever

Riders Of The Storm

Chaos flooded the streets. Thunder struck once more and I knew there was not much time left. The screams fell silent as an acid-green cloud of smoke filled the air. Silence fell upon the city and only I knew what would happen next. As I made my way through the foul-smelling smoke, I realised everyone had vanished. I couldn't see anyone within the city and the only sound which could be heard was the pounding rain echoing through the town. A blinding light suddenly illuminated the horizon... They were here...

Neve Warren (12)
Little Lever School, Little Lever

Unstable

I glare down in pride at the city I destroyed. I love the sound of screams. Also, the fact I know that buildings, containing many people, are crashing down. The house I was put together in, the one which owned my wires. The house I should destroy. The house I can't destroy. I don't care. Not one bit. I can't care! Not a little bit! The screams of agony sing like angles. I don't want to be careless, not one bit. I want to hear laughter, not screams, I want to save not kill. I want to shut down...

Abby Rose Barratt (12)
Little Lever School, Little Lever

Collapse

Crashing through the feeble structure of the falling building, the impaling current of the rushing tide. A cloud of white rolled throughout the land, taking all it collided with alongside it, wave after wave. The water ploughed through what was left of the hotel's complex, knocking down the remaining pillars and completely taking the building down the path of damnation, along with the people, struggling for survival, being thrown around inside their dull rooms, while those outside were taken in an instant.

Harrison Evans (14)
Little Lever School, Little Lever

Darkness

All I could see was darkness and hear screaming coming from the streets. I was horrified, I had no idea what was going on. I thought I was dreaming but it felt so real. Striding to the window, all I could see was black. Glancing at my phone I saw the time, 3pm. Horror, chaos, mayhem, a jagged fork of lightning sliced through the inky sky. A massive amount of people were outside then instantly it was gone and all I could hear was screaming. It felt like I was being tortured, I just wanted this nightmare to end.

Lucy Jones (13)
Little Lever School, Little Lever

The Vaccine

We just escaped the fort in the nick of time, my heart was beating as fast as a moving bullet. We were running from the criminally insane, they were fast and crazy but we were faster. It was a good thing that one of the prisoners was actually committed for a crime they didn't do and had made a vaccine to stop these walkers and turn them back to a human again. We put the vaccine in a very powerful flare gun and shot it into the air. The vaccine spread through the atmosphere and everyone became human again.

Callum Lane (14)
Little Lever School, Little Lever

Downtown

Nights in the city of Placetown can be rough. The winds are sharp and like daggers. Dark alleys are cluttered with criminals, waiting for their impending doom. An adventure lurks behind every awaiting corner. Mobsters congregate in boisterous bars, playing poker, which are filled with fraudsters who bluff for their wages. God forbid anybody goes bankrupt. Metal will be ripped out of pockets and fired mercilessly. Bodies fall to the ground like leaves in autumn. It is bound to be a busy week in the morgue.

Molly Walkden (14)
Little Lever School, Little Lever

The Bomb

After the bomb went off a couple of miles away in a town, he fell to the ground with a ringing in his ears. He looked around, he was a lucky one. Only a few survived. As soon as he cleared out, he heard nothing. It was silent. *How many bombs are left?* he asked himself. He noticed the mushroom head of the cloud. Covering his mouth, he dived into an empty darkness. As he regained his consciousness, he was in a helicopter with uniformed men. As they landed, they said everything was going to be okay.

Kian Walmsley (11)
Little Lever School, Little Lever

Villain

You think I want to be doing this? The answer is no. I look down at the burning, defenceless city beneath me, crumbling down into tiny, little fragments on the floor of what was once their home. I feel harmless as the gunshots are piercing through my armour, defeating me. The smell from the blazing fire blocks my nose and I am unable to smell the blood from the children that were once alive. I am that monster you see in films: the villain. Not the hero. Never the good guy, not after what happened to me.

Jessica Alice Ramsden (12)
Little Lever School, Little Lever

Nihil

As the threatening and menacing nightmares edged closer to the door, the thunderous screams echoed and intimidated the fragile lives that surrounded the great hallway. The terror paced closer until all the vulnerable people could only wait. Wait to live, wait to die. Darkness lingered whilst mothers painfully grieved and young children screamed, waiting for nothing, praying for nothing, hoping for the end to appear. The shrieks ended, the cries ended, their hope ended. There was nothing.

Caitlin Rhead (13)
Little Lever School, Little Lever

Mr Murder Man!

I looked down at the roaring fire, invented by the beaming lasers coming from my eyes. I remembered the past when I was calm but then he came and destroyed my family and now it was time for my revenge. Peeping over a balcony stood a man. He had a gun in his hand and wore black clothes. He looked as if he was the man. The man who destroyed my family's life, even my six-year-old girl. All of them, so dead he lay. Dead on the balcony. Dark red blood pouring out of his head.

Hanna Goodwin (12)
Little Lever School, Little Lever

Forgotten Times

The last warning shot rang out across the valley as a devilish cry of guilt echoed a once-arid landscape. A grieving mother cradled her lifeless bundle whilst the cacophony beneath shrieked in a sudden torrent of rain. Hunched over in fear, this vulnerable silhouette now only a distant memory by many lay on the blood-soaked floor as conflict surrounded her. Young children fled to the safety of the dense woodland surrounding as soldiers continued to murder innocent families.

Lucy Grime (14)
Little Lever School, Little Lever

The End Of Finch's 100 Runs

Afraid and terrified, the next ball from Mohamad Amir and Finch was waiting to hit the ball. Suddenly, a storm of dogs burst onto the pitch and it was the 23rd over and three wickets down. The ball went in the shirt of the batsman as the dog bit him. On 99th run, he needed to run to get his 100. Hundreds of other dogs bit him, he was dead on the pitch. He would be remembered in the history of cricket forever, as being 99 not out. For the Australian team to win the match.

Atta Rehman (13)
Little Lever School, Little Lever

Red

Blurred, everything is blurred. Except that one image that burned in my mind. Even so, not even that image was clear enough but I knew I couldn't stop here any longer because if I did it would find me. That was why I was currently running from it. I spun my head round to see that same beast who devoured this city of its life. Those glowing, red eyes were a reminder that there was no hope, sooner or later all I'd be seeing would be red, just red.

Grace Gavin (12)
Little Lever School, Little Lever

Zombie Apocalypse

We were the only ones left to save the world. I walked around the room. I wanted to save the world but I didn't know how. There was a zombie apocalypse. I had one gun. I wanted to be a superhero. I opened the door. Nothing was waiting outside. We ran to the roof. There was a helicopter waiting for us. All of my family got inside of the helicopter. I just needed to do the impossible. Down below, the ravenous zombies continued to spawn...

Naomi Barber
Little Lever School, Little Lever

The End Of The World?

The sky was clear, no clouds to be seen. The sun beamed in the sky. The day seemed perfect. Everything was about to change and nobody knew. *Bang!* Buildings crumbled like shortbread and enveloped all below. People scattered from street to street. Riots of people stampeded past me, towards the safety zone. Families were torn apart like paper and were scattered in the wind. Was this the end? Who would make it to the safety zone?

Mia Conway (13)
Little Lever School, Little Lever

The Demon Best Friend

The screams fell silent and nobody knew what happened except me. It was my best friend, Jess. The next day, we were walking home after a bad day, our teacher had given us detention. Jess started to become very angry. Soon, her eyes turned red, her nails turned to claws and wings grew from her back. In the blink of an eye, she was in such a rage, fire shot from her mouth. All the world was destroyed, all except for me and Jess.

Isabelle Greeney (12)
Little Lever School, Little Lever

Not Anymore

Angry, afraid, confused about what I was going to do. The traffic stood still. Staring at me: only me. I didn't care that I was a serial killer. I didn't care I was killing people, trying to get home to their families. I stabbed, cut, strangled, shot and a lot more things you don't want to know. My 'eyes' stared at the human soul lying dead on the floor. I was not human, they were not anymore...

Kelsey-Jo Frost
Little Lever School, Little Lever

The Hunt

A shadow lurked over the doorway, slowly creeping into the charcoal-black room. Waiting, watching, stalking for any helpless prey hiding in the shelter. Its footsteps echoed in the empty halls; its breathing was deep and heavy; its figure tall, distorted and mutilated; its face was ashen-white. Only a mouth that oozed with deep crimson blood was visible in the shrouded room.

It planted its tall, slender body on the spot and glared straight ahead, its jaws revealing an eerie, taunting smile etched across its once lifeless face. The person before it fumbled as it ran.

The hunt had begun...

Lucas Stephen Green (12)
Neston High School, Neston

Mission Chaos

The sun obliterated into pieces. Fragments of solidified fire launched across the globe. The Internet had shut off and telephone signals were no more. It was the start of the world's end. Many bodies lay cold and lifeless yet the heat was beyond scorching. The only light that remained were cars that had set ablaze. Helicopters and planes crumbled to the ground. People became demented and started stealing from shops, they threw bricks at windows and assaulted each other. Many committed suicide by running into fires or jumping from buildings. The man in the moon had turned on us all.

Alfie Elliott Fisher (13)
Neston High School, Neston

The Fatal Football Finale

Football. A game with such controversy, but this was no play in the park. The world's best had joined together to save the planet. The battle for survival had begun. The destiny of the planet would be determined by the winner.

Time stood still. The aliens went for a final attack. Our players had defended for our lives but it was to no avail as the ball flew into the net. Their exuberant faces contrasting with the despair of the whole human race as they concluded that the bountiful Earth as we know it would draw to a devastating end...

Ben Downham (12)
Neston High School, Neston

Them

They found us. They were coming, and no one survives them. All we could do was wait to die like the rest of the world. As they arrived, we heard them all around us. They were herding us like sheep in a slaughterhouse waiting to be butchered. I heard a sudden wince of agony next to me, but it was quickly silenced. They were picking us off one by one. That's when it happened. When my eyes got heavy and my throat started to close up. My arms swayed back and forth, I dropped. Then a bright light absorbed me.

Caroline Ross (12)
Neston High School, Neston

Untitled

Ash, all he could see and smell was ash. He laid outside the once-local bakery where he first met his wife. He remembered the day they first felt true love, yet now they laid there, close to unconscious, no longer feeling love, just fear. He turned to his wife who he had carefully placed on the weaved 'Welcome' mat that survived the apocalypse. Her hair was ragged, her clothes were dusty. Once they evacuated their home, she could no longer walk due to the agony caused by the disaster.
"Please!" he whispered through sobs. "Please don't leave me. Someone help!"

Olivia Florence Long (13)
St Julie's Catholic High School, Woolton

Everyone But Himself

He stepped out of the rubble that he once called home. The sign, scratched, broken, laid next to him: *47 Southbank Way, proud home of Mr J. Baker*, engraved strongly into the silver plate. John regretted this, killing everyone. That wasn't what he meant. Ushing through his head were the thoughts of selfishness that had led him to this ugly position. Five minutes. Running rapidly towards the nearest termination point, he dragged his wounded leg behind him. Four minutes. It was so close, yet so far. Three minutes, two minutes, one minute. He was too late. The empire had overcome.

Daisy Darmody (13)
St Julie's Catholic High School, Woolton

The Last Of The War Effort

I sprinted towards the bunker as the booming sirens went off. The laughter and excitement had now turned into screams, as bangs and booms went on. The war had begun. The few remaining soldiers from two countries had begun fighting with each other, this was because they thought they had started the chaos. Everything was going crazy. One... two... three... *bang!* More screams fell silent, more bodies on the floor, more lives taken. Soon there would be no more. Out of every situation, this was most deadly. I was sitting in the bunker, questioning, *will I survive or die?*

Ruby Kidd
St Julie's Catholic High School, Woolton

Dystopia Story

Wind. Rain. Fire. Hell. That's where she was trapped. From underneath the rubbled town hall, she could hear the weather hailing. She didn't dare go outside, for fear of being taken too. Taken by the thing that took her mother, her sister, her sanity. Suddenly, there was a *bang!* A bang on the door. She felt pure fear for the first time in a long time. But for a moment, a small moment, she felt comfort. Maybe she wasn't the only one left. She felt like this, only briefly, as very soon the fear came flooding right back to her.

Heather Langton (14)
St Julie's Catholic High School, Woolton

Abandoned

One cold, dark evening, I decided to stroll outside to watch the sunset and the moonrise. My usually busy street was deserted! Where were all the cars? The people? I decided to walk along to the park, but again, it was empty. I knew it had been on the news a lot lately, about people getting kidnapped, but surely not everyone.

"Follow me, I know you want to," an eerie voice whispered.

"What?" I screamed, maybe a bit too loudly.

The last thing I felt was a sharp tug on my shoulder. Now, I was gone forever.

Emma Robinson (11)
St Julie's Catholic High School, Woolton

Untitled

Chaos had taken over. The once-bustling city was no more. He laid outside in the middle of the road. He slowly walked over to the school at which he and his soon-to-be wife had met eight years ago. A million questions rushed through his head, *is she okay? Where is she? Will I ever see her again?* The apocalypse had started. Emma was nowhere to be seen. Tears streamed down his face, he slumped next to the school railings, thinking about the day that four words change his life.
"Will you marry me?"
It was a yes.

Amelia Leather
St Julie's Catholic High School, Woolton

Desolation

She skipped across the deserted streets, muffled cries and moans were only a distant echo in her ears. Memories of her old life danced like a ballerina throughout her head, but she shook them off faster each time. Her legs tired, her arms aching, her face groaning in pain. She pushed her way through the dead bodies that were lined up in her way. As she approached the top of the towering hill, her last hope of survival crumbled inside her heart as she saw the chaotic city from a distance, not even all humanity was strong enough to help.

Ava McCutcheon
St Julie's Catholic High School, Woolton

Test Subject

My mind scratched at the walls of my head as I tried to escape my thoughts and awaken my body. Panic rippled through me as I ripped my eyes open and my vision unblurred. I was hooked up to a machine and I heard the deep mumbles of people fade away. A heavy ache consumed me as I felt something shiny pierce through my torso. My eyes shut and I yelped, screaming in agonising pain. Images flashed through my mind of an erratic, hellbound and destroyed world. I could save everything, I was an experiment, the key, the sacrifice.

Caitlin Mottram (14)
St Julie's Catholic High School, Woolton

Conversation Needed

Three years. It had been three years alone and scared. Horrible thoughts swirled around my head but I chose to ignore them. I had to, otherwise I wouldn't be able to feed myself or make shelter. I grabbed my backpack and set out to look for any sign of life. This was now part of a daily routine because finding life meant I wouldn't be alone anymore and I would be able to have a real conversation with somebody. Thinking about this made me feel warm inside but it would last for only a second, and that kept me going.

Liv Ellis
St Julie's Catholic High School, Woolton

Untitled

The telephone rang in the rubble of a place that used to be a family home. I stumbled past the car alarms and howling dogs to reach the City Hall. Ever since the apocalypse started, the government had gained power and put new laws in place. One of which was that violence and murder were legal. Every Sunday, I got rations from the City Hall. It was a scary journey as I could be attacked any moment. I continued down the road when suddenly, a man shot my friend, Suzie. I ran. I was not safe here. Please send help...

Ava Dawes
St Julie's Catholic High School, Woolton

Not Gizelle

I ran, my baby, Gizelle, in my arms. Scared, not only for my life but for my baby's too. After miles of running, I took shelter under an old bridge that joined Richdale and Forbs together. I felt the ground shake as a bomb dropped close to me. The blast must have hurt Gizelle's ears, she started to cry. I told her to shut up or we would be found. There was silence. Then, I felt a strong blast next to me. I couldn't stand. Gizelle wasn't there, I called her name. There was no answer...

Lexi Russell
St Julie's Catholic High School, Woolton

YOUNG WRITERS INFORMATION

We hope you have enjoyed reading this book – and that you will continue to in the coming years.

If you're a young writer who enjoys reading and creative writing, or the parent of an enthusiastic poet or story writer, do visit our website **www.youngwriters.co.uk**. Here you will find free competitions, workshops and games, as well as recommended reads, a poetry glossary and our blog.

If you would like to order further copies of this book, or any of our other titles, then please give us a call or order via your online account.

Young Writers
Remus House
Coltsfoot Drive
Peterborough
PE2 9BF
(01733) 890066
info@youngwriters.co.uk

Join in the conversation!

 YoungWritersUK   @YoungWritersCW